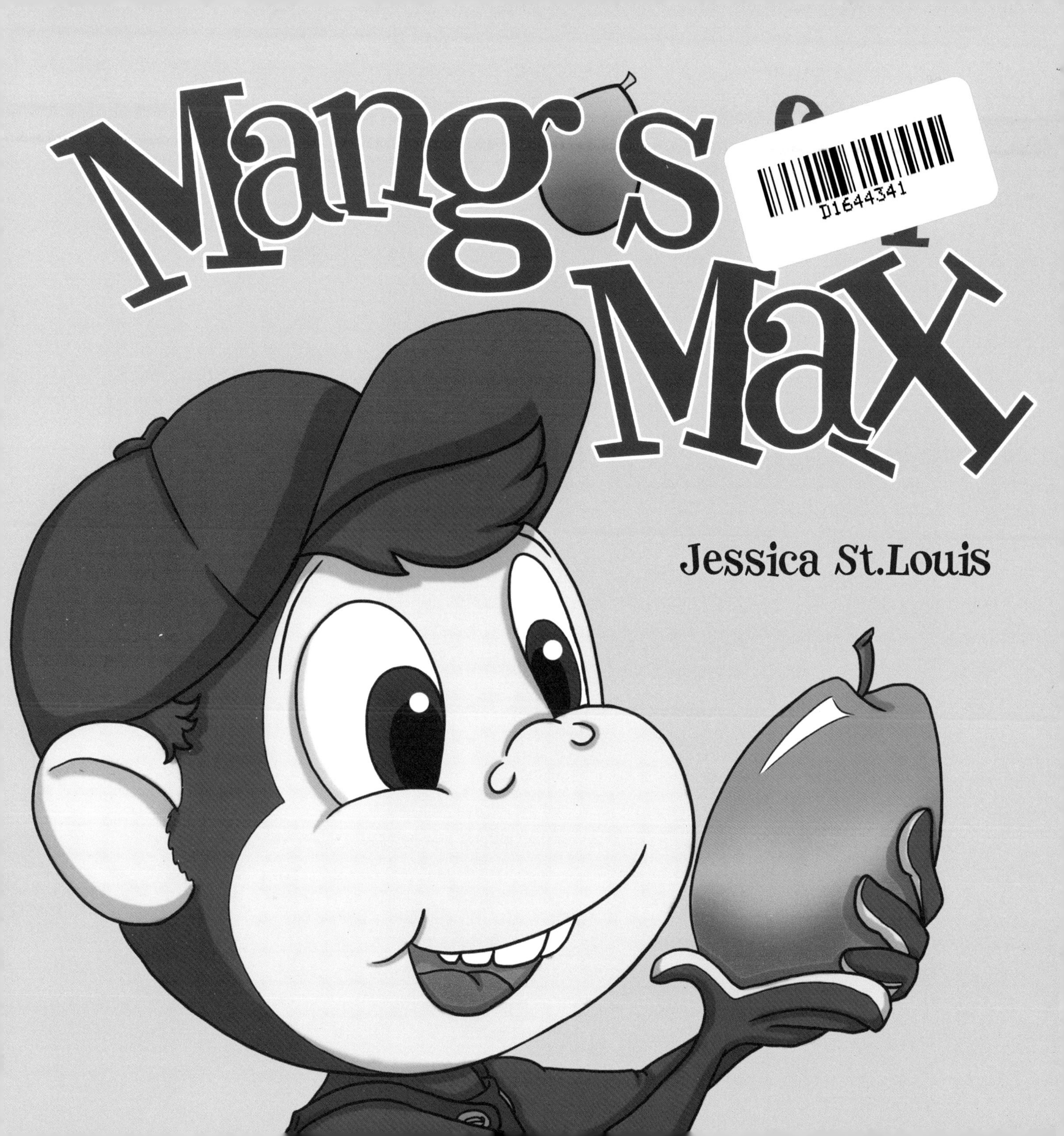
Mangos
Max
Jessica St.Louis

ISBN: 1477602070
ISBN 13: 9781477602072
Library of Congress Control Number: 2012910394
CreateSpace Independent Publishing Platform
North Charleston, South Carolina

For my boys.

M

DEEP IN THE JUNGLE, where everything is colorful and bright, lives a monkey named Max, who is silly each day and every night.

Max the monkey loves to play.

He jumps and runs every day.

Max can swing from tree to tree.

He is as happy as a monkey can be.

When this playful monkey spins around and around he sometimes goes so fast that he falls to the ground.

He walks on his hands all the way to school.

Max the monkey is super cool.

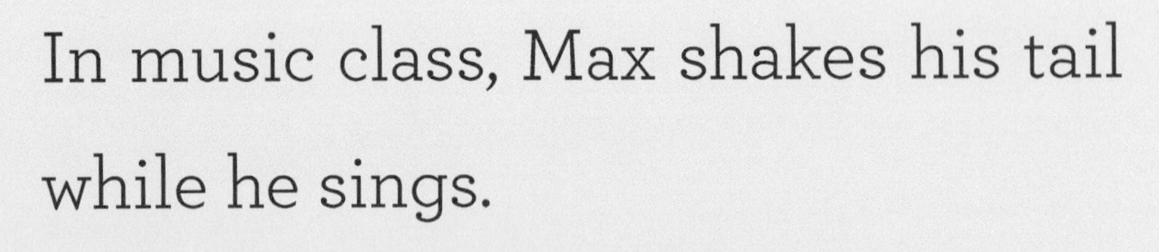

In music class, Max shakes his tail while he sings.
During recess, he hangs from the rings.

When the teacher says, “It’s time for snacks,” the monkeys wash their hands, including Max.

All the monkeys sit down really quick, but Max must be careful, because some foods make him sick.

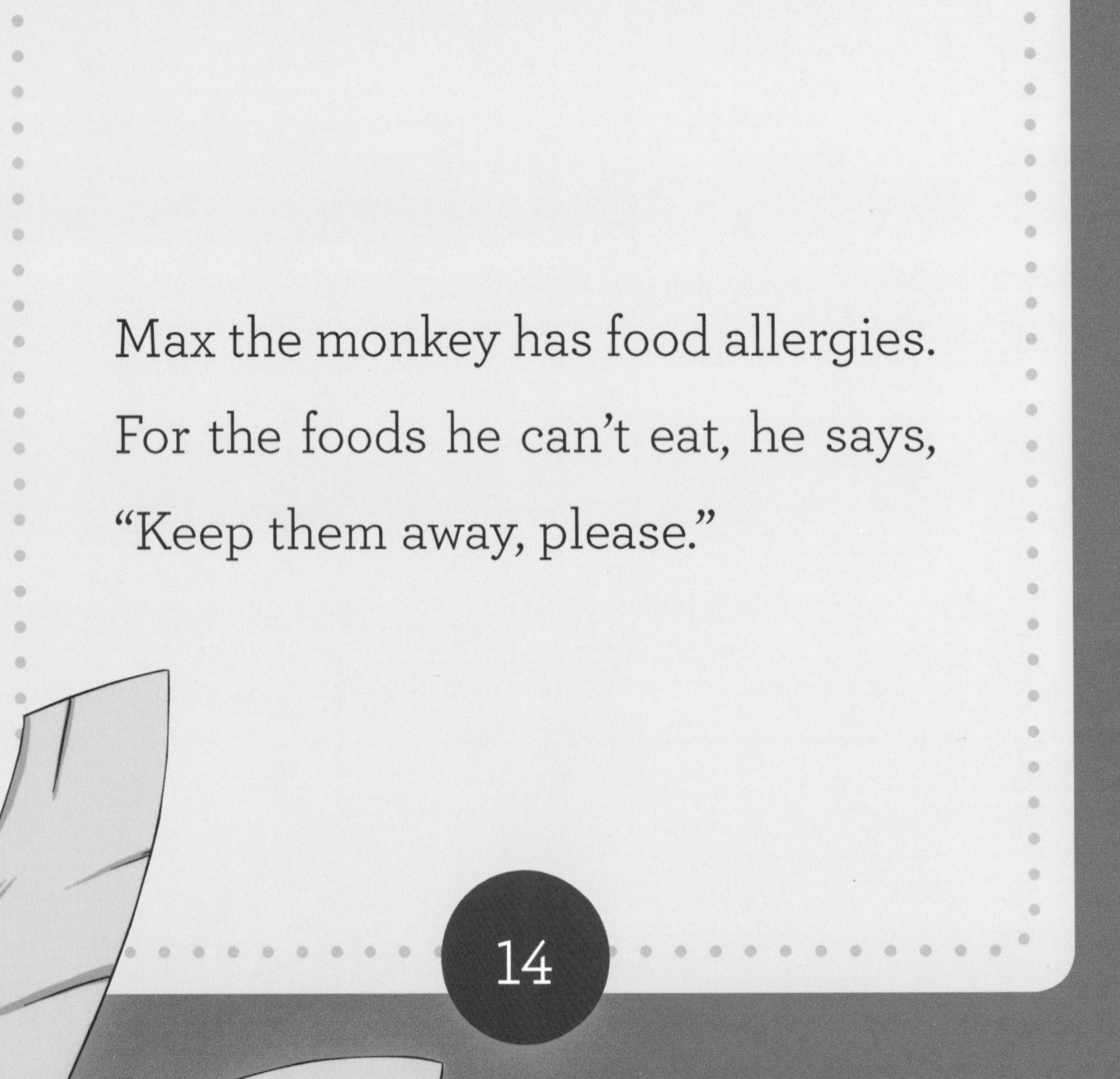

Max the monkey has food allergies.
For the foods he can't eat, he says,
"Keep them away, please."

Food allergies are nothing to dread. He knows what to eat after food labels are read.

While his friends eat bananas, Max eats mangos instead.

Max stays away from the foods of each friend.

This way everyone stays safe and happy in the end.

Now that snack time is over, it is time to go play.
All the monkeys are happy and safe, *hip hip hooray!*

Mangos for Max will donate 10% of all proceeds to further food allergy awareness and research by contributing to FARE.

Food Allergy Research & Education (FARE) works on behalf of the 15 million Americans with food allergies, including all those at risk for life-threatening anaphylaxis. This potentially deadly disease affects 1 in every 13 children in the U.S. – or roughly two in every classroom. Formed in 2012 as a result of a merger between the Food Allergy & Anaphylaxis Network and the Food Allergy Initiative, FARE's mission is to ensure the safety and inclusion of individuals with food allergies while relentlessly seeking a cure. We do this by providing evidence-based education and resources, undertaking advocacy at all levels of government, increasing awareness of food allergy as a serious public health issue and investing in world-class research that advances treatment and understanding of food allergies. For more information, please visit www.foodallergy.org

CPSIA information can be obtained at www.ICGtesting.com
Printed in the USA
LVIW01n1924080318
569140LV00008BA/89